my favourite things

A World Of Fun

Edited by Allison Jones

First published in Great Britain in 2009 by:

 Young**Writers**

Young Writers
Remus House
Coltsfoot Drive
Peterborough
PE2 9JX
Telephone: 01733 890066
Website: www.youngwriters.co.uk

Foreword

Young Writers' My Favourite Things is a showcase for our nation's most brilliant young poets to share with us the things they appreciate most in life.

Young Writers was established in 1990 to nurture creativity in our children and young adults, to give them an interest in poetry and an outlet to express themselves. Seeing their work in print will encourage them to keep writing as they grow, and become our poets of tomorrow.

Selecting the poems has been challenging and immensely rewarding. The effort and imagination invested by these young writers makes their poems a pleasure to enjoy reading time and time again.

Contents

Darlinghurst Primary & Nursery School, Leigh on Sea

Gayhurst School, Gerrards Cross

Limpsfield Junior School, Sheffield

Paible School, North Uist

St Mary Magdalen's CE Primary School, Accrington

The Poems

Lego Batman

I play on Lego Batman, it is a lot of fun
When I went on two player
I nearly almost won.

I am always Robin, he is really cool
But when he landed on his head
He really looks a fool!

When I fight the Joker, he is such a laugh
When I fight Killer Crock
I give him a big bath.

When I was on the last level
I nearly got to the end
But someone came in and I got distracted by my friend.

Jason Bramley (9)

History

History is my favourite thing.
History is a wise man's brain.
History is a viewing window into the past.
History is what shapes our world today.
History is like travelling back in time.
History is what makes my heart beat.
History is a person's past.
History is my favourite thing.

Miguel Suarez Jimenez (12)

My Favourite Things

Films and music, sun and light,
The love of your mum holding you tight.

The smells of the breakfast after a sleep,
Crackling campfires which make you want to leap.

Voices of children playing cheerfully,
The evening mist and not a person feeling tearfully.

A massage after a stressing day,
The sound of someone saying you don't have to pay.

The sound of all the nice kings,
These are my favourite things.

Elle Youngs (11)

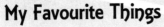

My Favourite Things

Things are just so fun
But what I think is just so great is playing in the sun,
Going to school,
Laptops and gadgets are just so cool,
Long, long holidays which are just so fun,
I like it when girls sing loud
And I just love reading.
I even love RE and history
But what I love the most is when my mum praises me!

Rea Sachdeva (8)

Favourite Things

Rattle, rattle, rattle, rattle
Mighty wooden roller coaster
Heaving up, racing down
And crashing through the bends.

Click, snap, click, snap
Fiddly little Lego bricks
Build it up, knock it down
Then build it once again.

Drip, drip, drip, drip
Rain against the windowpane
Howling blackened skies
The storm goes raging by.

Roller coasters, Lego bricks
And storms on a winter morning
All fill my world with happiness
My world of favourite things.

Robin Gwilliam (10)

My Caring Family

In my time on this planet I've learnt one thing,
That my family and friends are very welcoming.

If something went wrong, they'd be there for me,
They'd cheer me up and keep me company.

If a birthday and Christmas they weren't there,
My whole life would be completely bare.

Seeing my family is such a treat,
When I'm with them, I am complete.

And if any of them are feeling down,
I'll be there to turn things around.

Max Dervan (9)

My Favourite Things

Laptops and games and playing with my pet
Walks and talks and shooting basketballs in the net.
Going to school and being with my friends
These are a few of my favourite things.

Riding my bike and playing with my kite
Dancing and singing are the best
Being with my baby sister
Well, that just beats the rest!
These are a few of my favourite things.

Baking cakes and biscuits and things
These are a few of my favourite things
But best of all is being with my mum.

Courtney Hughes (9)

Girls

Girls are as gorgeous as a pink rose.
Girls are as shiny as shimmering shoes.
Girls are as clever as a clever clogs.
Girls are so pretty, boys go, 'Aah!'
Girls are popular.
Girls are as special as a sparkling star..

Lucy Beckett (9)

The Weather

Out on a snowy day
Everyone on sledges
Shouting, screaming
Having fun
Snowballs fly everywhere
Hitting trees
They crack their fingers in the icy frost
People dodge and twist
To avoid them
They think they don't like them
No one cares about his or her feelings
They just think that they're for climbing on
But everyone and everything has feelings
The pond is iced over
People think it's thick
Splosh!
Oh no! Someone's fallen in!

Lucy Draper (10)

9

Australia

The sun shone like a shimmering disco ball
Working day by day heroically like a mouse.
Through the lonely pavement,
I walked in fear of the sun.
It felt as if I was a criminal
Going for execution.
The sun was following me,
It knew my agony.
The pure beauty of the sleeping ocean
Caught my eye instantly.
The exquisiteness was irresistible
My expectations of this country changed from
Fear to exhilaration!
No person could not but be joyful
To this stunning view
There could be no better country other than Australia.

Ashan Abeywickrema (11)

Do You Like This Stuff?

I like ice cream with whipped cream and sprinkles on top,
How many flavours have we got?
Games to play on all day, if I have time I'll watch TV,
Going to the shops to buy girl things,
Missing class or having days off!
Acting and singing and not being tough,
Playing outside, netball, rounders, also some boy stuff!
Being in plays (but not showing off)
Kittens that are soft, cute and furry,
These are a few of my favourite things, do you like them or not?
I have many more things but I think that's enough!

Helen Roome (9)

Sisterly Love

Laura is my pretty sis,
She's someone I cannot diss.
I feel loved when she's around,
With her there I don't feel down.

I love her and she loves me
Our love is something you can't see
But we know it's always there,
Something we can always share.

My favourite thing is my sis
A moment with her I can't miss.
Our bond is stronger than a tether
We'll have each other forever.

Olivia Hammond (10)

Clip, Clop, Clip, Clop

Clip, clop, clip, clop riding my lovely pony
Clip, clop, clip, clop as lovely as can be
Clip, clop, clip, clop ribbons in her mane
Clip, clop, clip clop riding down the lane.

Trot, trot, trot, trot people stand and smile
Trot, trot, trot, trot hooves eating up the mile
Trot, trot, trot, trot this is my dream
Trot, trot, trot, trot making my face beam!

Canter, canter, canter wind in my hair
Canter, canter, canter faster if I dare
Canter, canter, canter jump to reach the sky
Canter, canter, canter I feel that I could fly.

Clip, clop, clip, clop going home again
Clip, clop clip, clop the end of our wonderful trek
Clip, clop clip, clop my arms around her neck
Clip, clop, clip, clop her stable is so cosy
Clip, clop, clip, clop my favourite thing is Rosie.

Jenny Bennett (10)

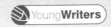

Christmas

Christmas is one of my favourite times
Flashing lights and Mum's on the wine!
Granny's cooked dinner; it's turned out a winner.
Mum's eating her dinner, she's getting no thinner
And having a glass of wine!
It's six o'clock, Doctor Who is on the box
We all sit down together
We have to agree, it's been a great day
While Mum sleeps off her dinner!

Jude Williams (8)

My Favourite Things

Football, football, the sport I love,
But the downside is the push and shove.
There are lots of other sports I do,
But not ballet, 'cause you wear a tutu!

I play squash which is really great fun,
It's basically like hit and run.
Anybody can play the sport at all,
All you need is a racket and ball.

Golf is another sport I play,
The weather's especially good in May.
When it's sunny the midges are out
They make you want to scream and shout.

When it's raining and I'm feeling blue
I think of something good to do.
I watch TV or read a book
But never ever do I cook.

Liam Thomson (11)

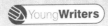

My Favourite Things

Shopping
Sweets
Flopping
Treats
Makeovers
Fun
Sleepovers
Sun
Swim
Laugh
Gym
Long baths
Family
And . . .
Me!

Audrey Woodhouse (11)

Favourite Things

Football and rugby,
Climbing through trees.
Running for miles,
Jumping the trapeze.

All of these sports I love to do,
But one thing that stops it is the flu.

Watching TV, PlayStation3,
Drawing the pictures that I like to see.

All of these things I love to do
Except watching the news for an hour or two.

Asking your mate over to play
Go down the park,
Stay there all day.

All of these things I love to do
Including writing poems for people like you.

Nathan Clarke (12)

17

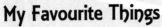

My Favourite Things

Hallowe'en and Christmas, reading a book,
Playing games, having a look.
Going on holiday, getting treats,
Playing with friends, having sweets.
These are a few of my favourite things.

Going shopping, family and friends,
Watching TV, playing with pens.
Birthdays, presents and ice cream too,
Having parties, the colour blue.
These are a few of my favourite things.

Cinemas, babies, lying in the sun,
Playing with my pet, having fun.
Listening to music, playing on my own,
Dancing about, not being all alone.
These are a few of my favourite things.

Natasha Greig (12)

What Makes Me Tick

Playing football with my mates,
Going down the bakers and eating cakes.

Seeing my sister learn something new,
Seeing her laugh and smile too.

3.00, the end of school,
Going swimming down at the pool.

Watching Cbeebies on a Saturday morning,
Lying in bed till the sun's long past dawning.

Eating sweets till my belly groans
Putting fingers in my ears while my mum moans.

Skiing down the black mountain
Throwing coins in the fountain.

Scrunching your face up while your dog licks
These are the things that make me tick.

Conal O'Neill (12)

Everything I Like To Do

I like kicking the ball into the net
I like meeting people I've never met.
I like playing on my Wii
You should really see me!
I like going to school
And acting right cool.
I like listening to my iPod
And I love eating cod.
I like reading Horrible Science
And playing Spiderman Alliance.
I like playing with my brother
And getting big kisses from my mother.
I like going to parties
And eating blue coloured Smarties.
I like laughing out loud
And I love being proud.
I like riding my mini moto
And having my school photo.
I like going on camps with the scouts
And I love it when we all shout.
I love watching TV
And eating kiwi.
I like going to the beach and having lots of fun
And I love it when my nan and grandad come.
When I am on stage I love to sing
These are a few of my favourite things.

Connor Stephen Silom (11)

My Favourite Things

M y favourite things are
Y ummy food

F easting on chocolate
A mazing views
V anilla ice cream
O ld English sheepdogs
U ndercover agents
R eally amazing things
I nternet
T alking about stuff
E ating pasta

T eddies
H alf term
I ce lollies
N apping
G iggling
S afety.

Rhiannon Hornett (10)

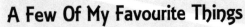

A Few Of My Favourite Things

Expressing myself in dancing,
Seeing the examiner glancing.
Playing my pink Nintendo, eating sweets,
Going trick or treating, collecting treats.
These are some of my favourite things.

Sparkling Christmas fun with my nanny,
French holiday sun with my granny.
Going to friends crazy parties
Eating cakes with pink Smarties.
These are some of my favourite things.

Hunting for my Easter eggs,
Seeing the Christmas stockings hanging on the pegs.
Cuddling up to my mum and dad too,
Hugging my brother even though he sticks like glue.
These are some of my favourite things.

I love to watch the glamour of X Factor,
I've always dreamt of winning a Bafta.
I like to think I am good at singing,
I love to hear the morning bells ringing.
These are some of my favourite things.

Aimee Kent (10)

My Cat Millie

My cat Millie is just the best
She's always having a rest!
She plays with me
Sometimes drinking my tea
But I love her to bits.

My cat Millie is always going to the loo
Millie even has a friend called Blue.
She gives me loads of cuddles
And sometimes drinks out of puddles
But she is just simply the best.

My cat Millie loves playing with frogs
And I think she dreams of driving her own quad.
She lounges about all day
And when she gets up we all shout, 'Hooray!'
But no matter what she does I'll always love her.

Leaha Clarke (11)

Dragonic Destruction

Lashing tail
Clicking claws
Razor teeth in crunching jaws
Fiery heart and fiery soul
Its lair, a cave as black as coal
Hypnotic eyes
Lethal wings
Towers it will topple
And knights it will fling
This is a dragon
And in a blaze of glory
Its battles are not gory
Since everything is gone
Ashes fleeing on the wind
The enemy disintegrated.

Amy Connor (13)

My Favourite Things

M is for muffins which are delicious
Y is for yeti who are very hairy

F is for fun which is school
A is for animals, especially otters
V is for vermin, some are cute
O is for Ola Jordan from Strictly Come Dancing
U is for Upton Warren which is totally awesome
R is for reindeer who look stunning
I is for Izzy who is my best friend
T is for tired at the end of a day
E is for eggs which are dyed at Easter

T is for teatime about five o'clock
H is of Hannah who has lovely hair
I is for icicles which are so dazzling
N is for nothing but fun
G is for golden Christmas lights
S is for super which last year was.

Amalie Coleman (9)

My Hobbies

I love drawing, sketching fantasies is what I mostly do
Like fire-breathing dragons and scary comic strips
With ghosts that shout, 'Boo!'
I also like reading, I have piles of books in my room
I like mythical things like bloodthirsty vampires and dungeons of doom.
I have a really cute pet bunny and she loves to skid about
Once she ate a whole cornflake packet
If I'd have done that, my mum would have given me a right big clout!
I absolutely love writing, just like I am now,
I've already had two stories published; one about a funny-looking cow!

Georgia Clarke (10)

My Favourite Things

Making a clean diving catch
Or hitting the boundary to win the match.
A sliding tackle that wins the ball
Which leads to our team scoring a goal!

The calm of the wide open sea
And flying along under sail, just the crew and me.
Chocolate and ice cream and sweets
And other delightful treats.

Doing well in maths and literacy,
Also languages, geography and history.
Passing a difficult test,
My score being one of the best!

Having a laugh and a joke
With all my best friends.
Having a hug with my dad and mum,
Altogether having good fun.

Going out in a tent into the wilderness,
Parties and birthdays, definitely Christmas.
Reading a good book and going out with family,
People recognising and liking me!

Cute little babies and getting a warm bed,
Friendly people and the nice things they've said.
All the latest gadgets like iPods and phones,
Making creative things in my nice home!

Philip Smith (11)

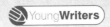
My Favourite Things

As the sun rises and the world awakens
The smell of the summer morning as a new day is dawning.
A smile from my sister and a hug from my mum,
These are a few of my favourite things.

As the hens cross, the dog starts to bark
The cat hisses and it makes me laugh.
These are a few of my favourite things.

Lauren and Aimee and Katherine and Shannon
These are my friends, we share all the trends
We go to the park before it gets dark
These are a few of my favourite things.

November, December, the snow starts falling,
Yes, snow at last, no school to go to.
These are a few of my favourite things.

Abiagil Culley (11)

My Favourite Thing

My name is Mollie Thompson and I really can't deny
That all the things in the world catch both my eyes.

I see them every day
I see them every night
I see them while I'm fast asleep
Tucked up very tight.

Butterflies and birds
Such a delight
Flowers and plants
A very lovely sight.

Cats and dogs
Fish and frogs
Animals' way up high
These are all my favourite things
That catch my very eyes.

Mums and dads
We couldn't live without
Sisters and brothers as well
But most of all these are my favourite things
Because they love us so well.

My name is Mollie Thompson and I really can't deny
That all the things in the world catch both my eyes.

Mollie Thompson (9)

Party Fun!

I went to a party yesterday, it was really fun
We played pass the parcel and guess what, I won!
Big balloons and banners and pressies for my chum,
Now it's time for food *yum, yum, yum!*
Fairy cakes and sausage rolls, crisps and chocolate too,
And those sour sweets that I really love to chew.
After lunch, it's time for cake, yummy, yummy, I can't wait
Make a wish one, two, three, cut the cake a piece for me.
I love parties, having fun, playing games with everyone.

Molly Hill (11)

I Love These Things

Hugs and kisses,
I love seeing my friend's snake that hisses.
Going on holiday with my best friend,
I wish it would never end!
Sticking things together
And giving them to Heather.
Eating ice creams
And at Christmas I love seeing beams.
Of course, while I am opening my presents,
And after we've been sledging, we see pheasants.
I love laptops and gadgets
And playing with my very adorable pets.
I love babies
But I hate rabies!
These are my favourite things.

Freya Jade Harding (10)

Ben's Favourite Things

My favourite things would start with my drums
Which I like to play with my very good chums.
Choosing a song and playing it over
I wonder if they could hear all the way in Dover?

My next favourite thing has to be cricket
When your friends will cheer when you get a wicket.
Batting, bowling and scoring runs,
Lowerhouse is my team and we score tons of runs.

My next favourite thing is special to me
As they are always stood right next to me.
These special people I always see,
As these special people are my family.

Ben Gorton (11)

Favourite Things

Singing laughing and dancing too,
These are the things that I love to do.

I open my mouth and let it run wild,
My answer is that I'm just a child.

I go to school and play dares with my friends
And go for wanders till the corridors ends.

I go to music, do keyboards again
One thing I hate is that I am partners with Ben.

He's a good friend though, I'll give you that,
Gym is next, yes we're on the mats.

I love doing gym, it keeps you fit,
But them all of a sudden my knee hurts a bit.

Shake it off and get back in the game
I don't want a big tick right next to my name.

Home time now, let's get on the bus
Laughing and shouting and causing a fuss.

A favourite thing is having a rave
I'm proper popular, my friends calling my name,

Love going shopping, it's lots of fun,
Going to the salon and getting my hair done.

These are the things that I love to do
Wake up in the morning feeling brand new.

I love being free as you can see,
These are the things that makes me, me!

Paige McDonnell (13)

33

Holiday Fun

Getting on a plane
On my way to Spain.
This is the start of my holiday fun.

I like to run
Under the sun
This is what I do for holiday fun.

Playing in the sea
Going out for tea
This is what I do for holiday fun.

Sitting on the sand
Listening to my favourite band
This is what I do for holiday fun.

Feeling like a fool
Going back to school
This is the end of my holiday fun!

Sinead Foley (9)

My Favourite Things

What are my favourite things?

Well . . .
I like sweets,
I like treats,
I like short skirts with pleats.
My boyfriend does too
But that's another story for you!

I like noise,
I like toys,
I like blond spiky boys.
I like diamonds,
I like rings.
I love to dance,
I love to sing.

I like drama
And English
And PE too,
But one thing I hate
Are maths lessons, *ewww!*

I like best friends
And boyfriends
And old friends
And new,
But I like especially
That person called you!

So as you can see
My favourite things are actually
Pretty much anything
Between you and me!

Abbey Kurton (13)

35

Henry

Having an education, learning at school,
Loving the fact that I know it all!

Stories to thrill, Indiana Jones,
I like the bit when they discover the ancient bones.

News reports, a police chase,
Or perhaps a nice drive at a reduced pace.

Car and bikes, mechanical engineering,
I do enjoy the satisfaction of fixing something.

Items of expense, iPods and mobile phones,
Having my favourite song as a ringtone.

But these won't do, no, they're not for me,
My favourite thing by far is playing with my hamster Henry!

Jack McGrath (11)

Hugs, Kisses, Love And Friendship

The soft touch of your embrace
Makes my heart swiftly race.
I feel safe in your arms
I will never come to harm.
The beauty in a world so sweet
Making our hearts skip a beat.
Love is such a beautiful thing
Without it our lives are nothing.
Friends are wonderful to be had
Cheering you up when you are sad.
They are with us always forever
And those true will hurt us never.

Chelsea Turner (15)

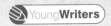

A Few Of My Favourite Things

A winged beautiful butterfly,
A white fluffy cloud in the sky.
Some very cute bunnies
And a sweet taste of honey.
These are a few of my favourite things.

An ice cream is a dream
When watching a fast-flowing stream.
The beach with the nice soft sand
Is always nice to the feel of a hand.

A few of my favourite things
Include diamond necklaces and rings.
I love the way the birds sing
About what tomorrow will bring.

It's such fun at an ice rink
But the memory ends within a blink.
Now it's time for a nice hot drink
These are a few of my favourite things.

I wouldn't know what's better
A summer's morn
Or a winter dawn.

On a summer's morn
You can lie on a green-coloured lawn
To watch the flower
Bloom with powers.

On a winter's dawn
You may see a galloping fawn
A newly fallen sheet of snow
Or a rabbit going into his burrow.
These are a few of my favourite things.

Fiona Tomkins (14)

Pink Lady

I really like my laptop,
She does a lot for us.
Although you need a password,
I never make a fuss!

Her skin is bright pink,
As pink as a rose.
With smooth silver keys
I see in the dark she glows!

You can make her nice and fancy,
Including a background and screen saver.
But forget all of them
Need to check mail on Messenger!

Playing games is next,
Which games shall I pick?
Action games or a puzzle,
I think I'll do a dip!

What shall I do now?
I really don't know.
Ermm . . . let me think,
Yes, I'll go on Bebo!

No, forget that, I'll type up a story,
What shall I do it on?
Pirates or fairies,
I don't know which one.

My story is fantastic
Says my mum
Dad shouts 'It's time to come off!'
As I shout, 'Dad, I'm not done!'

I really do like my laptop,
She really is the best.
Should I turn her off for a bit?
Yes let's give her a rest!

Anjali Patel (11)

My Favourite Things

My favourite things are special to me
Because my favourite things are where I like to be.
Horse riding, reading, writing and the sun,
Anything really, where I have fun!
I like to draw my dreams and colour them in,
I like to enter competitions and hope to win.
I like to go to the cinema and eat popcorn.
Really I can't choose my favourite thing of all.
My favourite things are special to me
Because my favourite things are where I like to be!

Adele Britnell (13)

Reading

R ound and round, meeting new faces
E xploring all the magic places
A dventures, mysteries, fantasy or horror
D rive to the library to get some to borrow
I n the lounge on the bed or in the bath
N ow you can read anywhere, even if it's daft
G etting to the end is sad but you can start a new one and be glad.

Sally Lancaster (10)

Favourite

We all have our favourite things,
The things you just couldn't live without.

Phone and gadgets are all the rage
Laptops and computers, put them in a cage.
They break so easily, like my arm,
Lots of money wasted, oh well, no harm.

Presents, TVs, gadgets, CDs, not all kids are so lucky.
Some living without mothers, no sisters nor brothers,
Living in places full of illness, poverty, disease and war!

We all should be equal, get rid of all greed.
We are born into one place, one world,
We are all human, all one race.

Favourite things shouldn't be pointless breakable technology
They should be precious memories treasured in your heart.
They don't break in the wind,
Nor do they get old-fashioned, they are yours forever.

We have a chance to change, have health, happiness, heart and soul,
We can make target and exceed our goals,
Able to touch, taste, hear, smell and see, use your sense more often
and let go of technology.

So keep those special memories,
Close the pictures, the words, the feelings, they aren't plastic
Unbreakable, untouchable, forever in your heart.

Memories, my favourite things
There even when you fall
No need for any money
That's why they are my favourite things of all.

Chloe-Louise Martin (13)

What Are Your Favourite Things?

Riding my bike and having lots of fun,
Going to the beach and sitting in the sun.

Sleeping in the garden, collecting lots of flies,
Watching Tracy Beaker and eating delicious pies.

Eid and Easter - treats and money,
Going to the park and mixing lots of honey.
Visiting the library, reading exciting books,
Doing something cheeky and letting off the hook!

A kiss from Mum, a hug from Dad too,
Going to school and making things from glue.
Listening to music and dancing about,
Drawing, reading and learning how to count.

Cats and dogs, hamsters and fish,
Going to a restaurant and eating a pasta dish.

Playing outside with my friends
Watching the calm sea of the River Thames.

Seerat Parvez (10)

But A Few Of My Favourite Things

PlayStation and Wii
Climbing a tree.
Covering my ears when my dad sings
Are but a few of my favourite things.

Watching football matches
While my grandma sews my ripped trouser patches.
And watching beautiful birds' wings
Are but a few of my favourite things.

Watching an ace DVD
My brother fighting with me.
Learning about superior kings
Are but a few of my favourite things.

Watching TV
With my best mate Lee.
Giggling at my mum's earrings
Are but a few of my favourite things.

Online gaming is such fun
So is sunbathing in the sun.
Racing home when the school bell rings
All these are my favourite things.

Ethan Wesley Stanton (8)

My Favourite Things

I like tennis, drawing, painting, eating ice cream, big diamond rings
But these are just a few of my favourite things.

I like chocolate, hugs from my mum and my dad too.
I like my pets, riding my pink bike and love it when Jack White and
Alisha Keys sing.
But these are just a few of my favourite things.

I like the X Factor winners, Leona and Alex.
I like watching TV, having fun, going on holiday with the family and
joining in at parties.
These are the things I like and I'm going to like forever.

Sophie Fishpool (13)

My Favourite Things

Imaging things
Grotesque creatures and fairies with gorgeous wings.
Jumping on my trampoline
Watching the peculiar episodes of Merlin.
These are a few of my favourite things.

Riding on my bike, now that is what I really like.
Going to a magnificent fair,
Meeting our quaint old mayor.
These are a few of my favourite things.

Going to amazing parks, visiting different landmarks
On a plane to St Lucia, travelling
Or maybe throwing my foam javelin.
These are most of my favourite things.

Watching a movie at the cinema
Listening to the singer, Lemar
Swimming or singing, family and me,
Snuggled up watching TV.
These are my favourite things.

Shanice Harris (10)

My Favourite Things

I like the sun when it shines
I like the moon in the sky
I like the summer days when I can play through
I like seeing the flowers grow in the summer days.

I like clocks that go *tick-tock*
I like sheep in a flock
I like fun and playing in the sun
I like treats and eating lots of tasty sweets.

I like sports, karate is best
My aim for the black belt is my quest
I like music, hip hop is great
But all types are cool
I listen when I celebrate
But most of all my favourite thing
The most important special thing
The greatest, treasured, beautiful thing is the love of my family.

Kelsey McKenna (11)

My Favourite Things

Flying to America to visit Disneyland
Going to the beach and playing in the sand.
Playing with my games especially my Etch-a-Sketch
Going out with my dogs and playing fetch.

Watching the animals short and tall
Listening to parrots loudly squall.
Making a mess in the kitchen whilst baking cakes
But every time Mum comes in and tells me off the mess I make.

Singing along to music R'n'B and pop
Funnily dancing along to hip hop.
Going to the pool and swimming underwater
Every Saturday just mother and daughter.

Watching SpongeBob and playing my DS
Eating all the chocolate is what I do best.
In the summer, in the garden is where I like to be
In the winter when it's cold, I like playing on my Wii.

Yasmin Langley (10)

My Favourite Things

Disco dancing la, la, la, goes the beat
I've got my funky shoes one
And my fave disco dress
Plus I've just had my hair down
You've gotta dress to impress
Because tonight's gonna be
A night to remember
Could you turn up the volume please?
Everybody I hope you're listening
Cos if you're not you'll be on your knees.

La, la, la goes the beat
I'm gonna dance till I can't feel my feet
I'm feeling the disco heat
La, la, la, la, la, la

I'm keeping on my smile tonight
Cos when I dance I give everyone a fright
And I'm eating up the disco ball light
You're scared cos you know I can
Do anything I wanna do, man!

When you dance you gotta lose yourself
Otherwise it ain't good for your health
Because you've gotta feel the waves
And then you feel like the waves are your slaves!

La, la, la goes the beat
I'm gonna dance till I hurt my feet
I'm feeling the disco heat
La, la, la, la, la, la.

Natahsa Okolo (11)

The Things I Love

Not much can beat the incredible feat
The thrill of the win, your opponent's defeat.
One of my favourite things is the win
Of a tae kwon do fight in the free-sparring ring.

One thing I do find is the joy of the mind
In reciting a piece of a very long kind.
To put on a show of piano or skit
And see the applause when the stage is all lit.

To travel abroad, see new places galore
Or watch summer clouds in the sky from the floor.
Climbing a tree or giving a hug
And steaming hot chocolate in your favourite mug.

The friendly face of a familiar place
My family and friends and my home are just ace.
And getting your poetry published of course!
These are my favourite things; tell me, what are yours?

Jordan Holmes (15)

My Favourite Things

I like animals and would love a pet monkey
Also a pig cos they look kinda funky.

Reading books about people and things
Listening to Girls Aloud when they sing.
Eggs and bacon and chocolate too
Yummy milk from cows which go moo.

Spaghetti Bolognese with sauce so juicy
Going to Build-a Bear with my friend Lucy.
There are many more things to the list I can add
But there is nothing more important than my mum and dad.

Caitlin Cochrane (11)

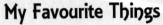

My Favourite Things

Playing in the garden, swinging on the swing,
Riding on my bicycle, I begin to sing
Then I spot a friend go by and make my bike bell ring.
Fluffy the rabbit runs on the grass,
She jumps and frolics and makes us all laugh.
I'm having friends round for tea,
So Dad goes off to light the barbie.
We jump on the trampoline and all have a laugh
At the end of the day it's bed after bath.

As I lie on my bed many things go round my head,
If tomorrow is dull and grey, I will stay in and play.
That's not a problem, I have lots to do
I'll make things with my craft sets and use a lot of glue.

I'll solve lots of puzzles and do colouring too,
Mum's friend will call and bring her baby,
Perhaps I'll have a hold, well maybe.
I may even try to ski on my new Nintendo Wii.
Oh my eyes are getting so heavy as I drift off to sleep
My favourite things in my dreams may now repeat.

Emily Lidgard (10)

Four Paws

I talk to her when I'm sad or alone
Because she's always there.
I can't talk to anyone else
Because they will only moan.
She sometimes just looks at me in a funny kind of way
And she always seems to have something to say.
I go to her when I'm upset
She always has a paw to lend.
She's not just my pet dog
She's my very best friend.

Georgie Leach-Clarke (12)

My Nanna — My Favourite Person

My nanna loved a lot of things
She loved shopping for shoes
Mugs books and diamond rings
My nanna also loved gardens and flowers
But she was still a fighter and was full of power
Also she was cheerful, active and funny
And loved things that were worth not a lot of money.
Nanna was caring, loving and kind
Nanny protected me; she was full of character that filled up the room
Some precious memories she's left behind.

Jesika Smith (13)

The Smell And Sound Of The Morning

The beaming of the sun in the morning
The smell of burnt toast
The sound of GMTV as I slope downstairs
Brother and sister arguing over what to watch
Mum shouting at them
The scraping of chocolate going on to toast
The rush of people getting ready for work and school
The slamming of the car doors
The sound of *chitter-chatter* as school kids walk past.
That's what I like to hear and smell in the mornings.

Hannah Metzger (12)

I Loved Being A Baby

When I was a baby, I felt fresh and new
And the centre of attention too.
My family cherished, love and constantly hugged me.
Visitors squeezed my cheeks mostly.
I became more anxious as I grew
Learning more things too.
I was a princess in my own world
Then I tried to bake a cake in the radio.
Then my time had come to grow up
And that included the washing up.
I enjoyed being a baby
Because it made me feel so lazy.
My favourite thing as you know is being a baby!

Gifty Brown (10)

Sweet, Sweet Surprise

Flapjacks, chocolates, sweets and more
Hotdogs, burgers, fries galore.
Gross, grey gravy on my plate
I'll try and feed it to baby Kate.

I like make-up, tops and skirts,
Size one shoes, ouch that hurts!
Bangles, bracelets, belt and bows
I'm so girly but no one knows!

Jenny Clark & Amy Nolan (10)

All My Favourite Things

I have two rabbits called Bread and Butter.
I have a dog called Daisy with eyes that flutter.
I have a tortoise called Toby, he is very small
And I've had so many goldfish I wouldn't count them all.
But Thomas my first rabbit was my best friend
I loved him lots till the very end.
I enjoy all the happiness that the bring
Because they are all my favourite things.

Katy Hole (10)

One Winter's Day

In winter I see
Snowmen sparkling in the snow
Trees that are bare
Snowballs being thrown
All around.

In winter I hear
Children shouting
Snowballs crashing
Wind blowing
All around.

In winter I touch
Wet snow melting
Soggy snowflakes
Cold icy water
All around.

In winter I feel
Warm and snug in my hat and coat
Freezing cold outside
Nice and warm when I am inside
All around.

I winter I smell
Warm hot pudding
Log fire
Christmas dinner
All around.

Lucy Victoria Whybrow (10)

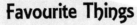

Favourite Things

Reading books, playing in the sun,
Going to a party having lots of fun!
Dancing around when my fave band sings,
These are a few of my favourite things!

Having lots of fun
Playing in the snow making salt dough
Dancing in the rain, people say I'm insane!

Pokémon, Disney, cute cartoons too
Going on rides in theme parks - but only a few!
Writing stories about fairies with big white wings
These are a few of my favourite things.

Fasiha Farzand (11)

My Favourite Things

The crispness of apples upon my tongue
And the sweet mellow juice of the watermelon,
The smell of the trees and their sticky red sap,
Skiing the mountains and popping bubble wrap.

The crackling of a fire in a warm open grate,
Watching South Park and staying up late,
Riding on camels and exploring,
These are the things that are interesting.

The crunch of sweet biscuits and the tang of good cheese,
Cool pickled onions and all that I please,
Watching my toast until goes *ding!*
These are a few of my favourite things.

Richard Ward (12)

My Favourite Things

Going to my caravan at the end of the week,
Riding on my new bike and getting loads of sleep,
Playing Mario Kart and beating my little bro,
Going to the park and me and Daddy teaching him to throw.
Making lots of yummy pink cakes with Mummy,
Laying on the warm grass when it's hot and sunny,
Getting lots of hugs and kisses, and tickles on my tummy,
Going to restaurants and eating nice dinners,
But they're not as good as my favourites cooked by Mummy.
But my most favourite thing of all is my baby sister, Ronnie,
And when she smiles at me it makes me feel very special
and bonny!

Stevie Herbert (10)

All About Me!

I love ice cream and football
And swimming and dancing,
Because they are the best.

Sweets and chocolate are so yummy,
I love to get them in my tummy.

Hip hop music is so cool,
Everybody plays it at my school.

Bags and shoes and hats and clothes . . .
This is where my money goes.

All these things come at a cost . . .
But without friends and family, I'd be lost!

Alix Lancaster (12)

My Favourite Things

Singing and dancing,
Sleeping and prancing,
Laughing and bending,
Saving and spending,
Cooking with mixtures,
All kinds of pictures,
Writing and talking,
Running and walking,
Drawing and reading,
Creating and leading.

Sian Dodd (11)

What I Love Doing

Eating lots of snacks,
Showing off my six-packs,
Watching TV all day,
Making stuff with clay.

Playing football regularly,
Making people happy,
Having lots of snowball fights,
Playing hide-and-seek all night.

Watching scary movies,
Eating lots of Smarties,
Cooking lots of nice things,
Running around for nothing.

Eating tonnes of ice cream,
Working as a team,
Listening to music,
Showing off in public.

Getting in trouble
For silly things like throwing pebbles,
Eating lots of spaghetti
In front of my mum and aunty.

Writing poems about my favourite things
Because I'm a talented young writer.
Thank you for giving me the opportunity,
Hopefully I'll see you later.

Saruphar Sakthivel (11)

My Favourite Things

Oh how I love Christmas,
To hear the Christmas bells ringing,
Or to go to mass
And listen to the choir singing.

Or Hallowe'en,
To go for 'trick or treats'
And find out who wins
The prize for the best sweets.

Maybe, perhaps I should say Easter,
Decorating the Easter eggs,
Having a fiesta
And taking drinks from kegs.

What about the summer hols?
They are just the best!
Maybe when we go to Seoul
And have plenty of rest.
These are just a few of my favourite things.

Cynthia Okoye (12)

Fun Things And Family

Our cat, Yoghi, who I loved so much,
My hamster, Toffee, so soft to touch,
Herbie the hedgehog with a soft wet nose,
Ollie the owl, who likes to doze.

I love the cut and thrust of fencing,
Rehearsals, rehearsals for the art of singing,
Tennis is my favourite sport,
Jazz dancing, a new activity I am taught.

Most of all, my brother comes first,
For Mum and Dad, so much love I'm fit to burst.
All these things are important to me,
Especially my family!

Lydia Thomas-Emberson (11)

The Stuff I Like

Movies, comics and racing cars,
And most of all I like KitKat bars.

Snickers bars and Ferrari cars,
Nothing makes a difference any more.

And I can't forget Marvel heroes,
And the bad villains always become zeros.

Oh and I could never, ever, ever forget,
Imaginative story writing.

Rajiv Jadav (8)

My Favourite Things

I like my DS and my cat Bess,
I enjoy watching James Bond films.

It's great when I listen to Amy Winehouse,
But my world's best thing is
My family and friends,
Because I love them!

Lawrence Burkitt (9)

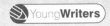

The Day Of A Lifetime!

Sunny days by the sky-blue sea,
Dancing and singing, or just being me.
Ballet, modern and tapping my feet,
Sometimes drama, which is a big treat.
Snowy weather - snowmen galore,
And when the rain starts to pour,
I hug my mum, I kiss my dad,
When my brother and sister are going to go mad.
When grandpa visits,
When my friends come to stay,
A really big party,
Hip hip hooray.
A holiday abroad,
New friends to meet,
A massive great villa,
Ice cream to eat.
Little babies -
Pink, sweet faces,
Tiny hands,
Lots of laces.
Loads of cake and lots of sweets,
Christmas presents, chocolate, sweets.
Painting, writing and reading a book,
Lots of cooking; I'm a good cook.
Cats, hats and lying on mats,
One more thing, I hate bats!

Eléonore Organ-Jennings (11)

My Favourite Things

My favourite things are
Playing in the sun catching things with wings,
Holidays and fun.

Also Hallowe'en and Christmas,
Eating ice cream and sweets
And getting presents and treats.

My favourite things are kissed from my mum,
A hug from my dad too,
And making stuff out of coloured paper and glue.

Also laptops and gadgets and playing with my pet,
Also scoring a goal a the back of the net,
And all of these are my *favourite things*!

Moynul Uddin (11)

71

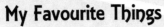

My Favourite Things

Laptops and games and playing with my pet,
Walks and talks, shooting basketballs in the net,
Going to school and being with my friends,
These are a few of my favourite things.

Riding my bike and playing with my kite,
Dancing and singing are the best,
Being with my baby sister, well that just beats the rest,
These are a few of my favourite things.

Baking cakes and biscuits and things,
There are a few of my favourite things,
But best of all is being with my mum!

Courtney Hughes (9)

My Favourite Things To Do

Ice cream and jelly on a hot summer's day,
Riding my pony, just watch him neigh,
Playing basketball in the sun,
Bouncing on the trampoline and having fun,
Hanging about with my best mate,
Cooking a meal that tastes great,
Watching a movie while snuggled up in bed,
Visiting my grandad, whose name is Ted,
Painting a picture and hanging it on the wall,
Beating my dad at a game of pool,
These are my favourite things to do!

Jasmine Turner (12)

My Favourite Things

Well . . . one is dogs and rabbits,
And different kinds of animals,
Learning about Egypt,
With the pharaohs, pyramids and camels.

Also a good book,
Any type really for me.
Hanging with my friends,
For they're kind and funny.

Seeing SpongeBob SquarePants
On the TV,
Or putting on
An animal documentary.

Doing well at school,
Learning new things,
But I have to say at the very least,
Homework's so boring!

Chillin' in my room,
Playing with my toys,
Not being a girly girl,
But messing with the boys.

But I think the very best of all
Is spending time with family,
For they are all so special
And make me so very happy.

These are my favourite things,
There aren't any more,
They are things that are lots of fun,
The things I'm grateful for.

Emily Thompson (10)

My Favourite Things

Playing the piano is something I do,
Acting, dancing and gymnastics too.
I play hockey, netball and do swimming quite a bit,
These things are awesome, you should try it!

At home I play with two monkeys, the twins,
I race in the garden and hope that I win.
At night, I love to go to sleep,
Although by the time I get up, my family are just about to eat!

School I go to every day,
I'm in the choir, I could sing all day,
I love reading books and drawing with paints,
Learning about kings, metres, verbs and saints.

Ice cream, chocolate, strawberries and cakes,
Feeding ducks who swim in lakes,
Though, to try something new,
Is the best thing you can ever do!

Annabel Ilic (10)

The Queen And I

My queen and country I truly love;
The bravery of our courageous heroes,
Trying to find peace symbolised as a white dove,
As it glides away like a long-lost doe.
But still there is something I love more so,
That cannot be put in so many words.
Can memories be named as an all time low?
Is it possible to take the songs out of birds?
More than the clouds, the moon, a star,
More than money and a Shakespearean play.
And so the purposes of my writing are:
For there is nothing in the world so dear to me
Than my beloved friends and family.

Emily Graver (14)

My Favourite Things

F ish in tanks and going out
A long with my friends
V egetables and meaty foods
O ut eating never ends
U sing the Internet and playing games
R eading really good books
I gloos, snowmen in the snow
T elevision all about crooks
E ggs, beans and bacon

T oys and all fun things
H appy thoughts and smiles
I ntelligent queens and kings
N ice and kind people
G irl or boy
S o many types of fish and that includes koi.

These are some of my favourite things,
All of these and more.
And when I go to bed at night,
I'll dream of these I'm sure.

Brandon Beaumont (12)

77

A Few Ways I Have Fun

These are a few ways I have fun:
By playing with my brother's toy gun,
I enjoy tormenting my brother
And reading the texts Mum sends to her lover.

These are a few ways I have fun:
Eating ice cream in the sun,
I like being nice
And scaring my mum with mice.

These are a few ways I have fun:
By eating a special iced bun,
I like listening to my favourite song,
And having a game of ping-pong.

These are a few ways I have fun:
Going for a nice long run,
I like to read and write,
But it's getting late, goodnight!

Ashleigh Sanderson (11)

Happiness Is . . .

A roaring hot fire
On a cold winter's day,
A holiday in summer,
Where I play near the bay.

In autumn, oh yes,
Leaves crunching 'neath my feet,
And then in spring,
The cute baby sheep.

Popping popcorn,
The telephone ring,
The tick of the clock,
When the blackbird starts to sing.

Crackling bacon,
Freshly washed clothes,
My mum's brand new perfume,
The smell of the rose.

All these things
I do so much love,
From the flowers in the ground
To the birds high above.

Tamsin Fletcher (10)

My Favourite Things

Hopping, jumping and watching TV,
And having people smile at me.
Dancing with mates when The Saturdays sing,
These are some of my favourite things!

Reading magazines and a good book,
Or going to my favourite shop, New Look.
Shopping for clothes, shoes and rings,
These are some of my favourite things!

Having a great time in the sun,
And after eating a sugary bun,
Drawing and scribbling, things that ding,
These are some of my favourite things!

Riding on my bicycle straight through town,
Then bouncing on my trampoline, up and down.
Hugging my sister, she really clings,
These are some of my favourite things!

Being eco-friendly and saving the planet,
I love doing this with my best friend, Janet.
This helps all the animals, especially those with wings,
These are definitely some of my favourite things.

Chloé Cuthbertson (12)

My Favourite Things

The soft, sweet cream and the coffee taste
Which my tongue amongst it all has traced
Of tiramisu, my favourite dessert.

The goggly eyes and gentle smile,
His tentacles are in curly style,
The irresistible piglet squid.

Into the hoop goes the ball,
The crowds are screaming out and call,
What a very wonderful goal.

But the things that are the best,
So much better than the rest,
Are my lovely friends and family.

Georgia Gibson (10)

My Favourite Things

My warm bed when I wake up is as comfy as can be
And Daniel, my kid brother, is so cute as he's just three.
I love my DS and I love Nintendo Wii,
And a very favourite pastime is watching TV.

Football, swimming and karate are some things I like to do,
Camping with my family and friends is lots of fun too.
I like to play and wrestle with all my mates,
Day trips out, a sandy beach and summer fêtes.

Birthdays, Easter and Christmas score very, very high,
I love receiving presents from that jolly Santa guy.
Pizza, sweets and chocolate are great to eat,
Coke and lemonade sometimes for a treat.

All these things are special,
All these things are cool,
But I would be telling a bit of a fib
If I said my favourite thing is school!

Thomas Black (9)

My Favourite Things

Beauty and music, sunshine and light,
Going on holiday but hating the flight.

The smell of the morning after summer's rain,
Watching parents open a cracking bottle of champagne.

Voices of little children singing songs of joy,
Playing around with their little toys.

The changing of seasons, a moment of prayer,
Goosebumps and laughter, my favourite chair.

Being lost in a moment, the voice of a friend,
Being held in a hug I hope never ends.

Going outside, enjoying the sun,
Listening to your CDs, a moment of fun.

Sincerity and honesty, faith, hope and love,
Knowing that God is somewhere above.

The presence of angels, a wonderful dream,
Having a lick of strawberry ice cream.

A kiss from your mum, and your dad too,
Thinking of all the things you've been through.

X Factor, Disney Channel, watching all that,
Maybe playing with your dog or your cat.

Sharing a secret, shouting out loud,
Laying back in the sun guessing shapes in the clouds.

Rain on the rooftop, silence so still,
Running, sliding down a really steep hill.

The power of prayer, uninterrupted sleep,
Making a promise I know I will keep.

Sitting and thinking of my favourite things,
Like cupcakes and flowers and angels' wings.

The innocent sweetness of love's first kiss
And simply sharing my thoughts with a friend like this.

Holidays, consoles, playing around,
Sitting on the beach listening to the waves' crashing sound.

Rhys Rogers (14)

Stormy Seas

White horses crash violently over the rocks
then recede sharply, regretfully to their domain;
Galloping wildly they surge again,
with no visible solution of restraint.
So loudly the untameable beasts roar,
angered by sins unknown;
Pounding with superhuman force,
relentlessly surging and seeking to destroy.
In the charcoal sky the clouds tumble and clash,
shouting their anger to those who will listen.
Fire strikes down, illuminating the smothering darkness,
powerful,
beautiful.

The darkness in the sky disperses,
tranquilly, the opal moon shines,
bouncing mysterious light off the slate surface of the sea.
The rampaging beast quietens, mesmerised by the opal,
glittering itself with the beauty of black sapphire.
As the sun begins to rise in the east,
changing black sapphire to shimmering incarnadine,
I continue to watch in awe this spectacle.
To witness the clean power of nature.
To view only true and pure beauty.
My favourite occurrence that I shall encounter,
the storm.

Lucy Neat (15)

My Favourite Things

Cards and paper, bits of string,
I love to make everything.
Cards and letters, drawings too,
But once I've done, it's half-past two!

Dogs and cats are lots of fun,
Playing in the garden beside the sun.
Fluffy and soft they can be,
But sometimes they are bristly!

Singing and dancing are best of all,
Except for when I trip and fall.
When I do it, I shy away,
If I could, I'd do it all day!

Hannah Pickering (11)

My Favourite Things

My favourite things are food and animals,
I think about them all the time.
The thing I find the hardest though,
Was to make them rhyme . . .

One day I went to Tesco
And bought a ripe banana,
Then I tripped up on my front step
And it was eaten by my iguana.

My mum went in the kitchen
And cooked my favourite dish,
I accidentally tripped over my cat
And landed in a tank full of fish.

I was walking through the jungle
And I found a bunch of grapes,
I accidentally dropped them,
They were then squashed by loads of apes.

I was cooking a lemon meringue pie,
I was putting on the lemon curd,
Then suddenly through the cat flap
Came a flying bird.

I was sitting in my garden,
Eating a Double-Decker,
The trees started to wobble,
Then out came a noisy woodpecker.

Zoe Tilley (11)

Favourite Things

Expensive jewellery and high brand named clothes,
Helping people sort out their problems,
Reading long books and making up stories!
These are a few of my favourite things.

Going shopping and talking with friends,
Listening to music and watching TV,
Talking to friends on instant Messenger and Facebook,
These are a few of my favourite things.

Restaurants and parties,
Holidays and sleepovers!
Going to the park for bike rides with friends,
These are a few of my favourite things.

Ice skating and going on the trampoline!
Doodling on school books
And going to the cinema!
These are a few of my favourite things.

Baking with my brother and eating lasagne,
Going to concerts and doing some sewing,
Arranging flowers and designing clothes!
These are a few of my favourite things.

Raenée Awoonor-Gordon (13)

87

Pets

Pets are best,
You stroke them,
You feed them,
You walk them,
You *need* them,
That's what I think.
Pets are a pest,
You clean them,
You walk them,
You train them,
You talk to them,
That's what they think.

If I could have a pet,
A dog would be the best, not a pest,
For they are the loveliest.

This is my favourite thing
Kerching!

Francesca Green (10)

These Are A Few Of My Favourite Things!

Eating ice cream in the sun,
Playing in the garden and having fun,
Watching movies about queens and kings,
These are a few of my favourite things!

Playing with my friends when I'm feeling down,
And going for a shopping trip all around town,
Dancing when Girls Aloud or Rihanna sing,
These are a few of my favourite things!

Making a snowman on a snowy day,
Playing in the sea when we go on holiday,
The smell of cooking doughnut rings,
These are a few of my favourite things!

Fresh, crispy sheets on my bed,
A really gripping book that I've read,
The frothy chocolate milk that my mum brings,
These are a few of my favourite things!

The long, hot summer days with the sun in the south,
Space dust popping in my mouth,
A beautiful butterfly fluttering its wings,
These are a few of my favourite things!

Kelly Davies (11)

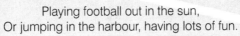

My Favourite Things

Playing football out in the sun,
Or jumping in the harbour, having lots of fun.

Spending time with my family and friends,
Or playing outdoors till the day ends.

Shopping with my mum,
Or ice skating and falling on my bum.

Going on a camping holiday
Or writing creative stories all day.

Reading my favourite book
Or getting into trouble and let off the hook.

Whatever life brings,
These will always be my favourite things.

Charlene Pitt (13)

My Favourite Things And Dislikes

I like maths,
But I don't like bats,
They remind me of cats,
And I don't like cats.

I like summer, messing about
In the paddling pool.
Don't be a fool, come along
And sing with us, it's very, very cool.

I don't like the rain, it is a pain,
It drowns away our play, hey, hey, hey.
I like the sun better, it shines all day,
It makes me smile, so the sun can stay while I play.

These are a few of my favourites.

Chloe Hargreaves (8)

91

My Best Things That I Like

My best things are messing with strings,
I love the swimming pool, now that is cool.
I like to pat my cat,
I love my house, even my pet mouse.
I also like clowns and visiting towns.
I like to bake a cake.
I like going to school and being creative with my tools.
I like eating a bun, whilst playing in the sun.
I like it when my dad sings
But they are all of my favourite things.

Khaled Saafan (9)

My Favourite Things!

My favourite sport is running
And also football too,
So when I'm with my friends
We have plenty of things to do.
I love going to parties with my family,
Or going to the cinema when I've decided what to see.
I like playing my DS,
And I like playing my Wii,
Then my little sisters come and ask to play with me.
My most favourite thing
Is that I really like to sing,
And after entering 'Britain's Got Talent'
I wait for Simon Cowell to ring.
I enjoy writing poems at school,
One of which got published in a book.
I showed it to my teacher and she enjoyed having a look.
I've always wanted a laptop so I'm sending this to you,
In the hope that I get chosen, so my dreams will all come true.

Fiona Boyd (11)

Me

I am a young boy from Bourne,
Who loves playing out on the lawn.
I ride my bike and fly my kite,
While eating my yummy cream horn.

I like to watch TV in my spare time,
While drinking lemonade and lime.
I play outside with my friends,
While having a very fun time.

I love my mum and dad too,
I play with them - there's lots to do.
We play lots of games and splash around when it rains,
But it's great when we go to the zoo!

Connor Boardman (11)

Alphabet Of My Favourite Things

Art and designing with a pencil in hand,
Ballet and twirling to the sound of a band.
Chocolate and sweets - my sis always chokes.
Dad, a person full of laughs and jokes.
English and learning new words every day.
Flowers and scents keeping dullness at bay.
Georgina, my sis, from Planet Hullaballoo,
Hanging out with friends, shopping together too.
Italian holidays, enjoying the sun while back here it's colder,
June, yeah! I'm one year older.
Katrina, my lifelong friend.
Learning new things and my knowledge I extend.
Mum kisses me goodnight and wishes me well,
Nestling into bed, now on the day I shall dwell.
Opening a pressie, I hope it's not a glove.
Painting with pink, a colour I love.
Queens in my history class, how did they rule?
Running to the changing rooms, soon to be in the pool.
Shopping for sleepovers, I'll take some Minstrels.
Toppings on ice cream, chocolate and sprinkles.
Universe poster on the wall.
Very cute kittens playing with a ball.
Writing a story with a villain who'll sin.
X Factor, who's going to win?
Yapping dogs playing in the park.
Zebras at the zoo, it's like Noah's Ark.
These are a few of my favourite things.

Chloe Hancock (12)

My Rabbit

My little bunny,
Eyes on the sides of his head,
He sees to the left and right,
Behind me and ahead.
My little bunny,
These are his long ears.
They help him hear many sounds,
He can hear from far and near.
My little bunny,
His strong legs are for jumping,
Warning others of danger
He uses his feet for thumping.
My little bunny
With a black and fluffy tail,
He lifts it up into the air,
Bunnies now follow his trail!

Oussama Moussaid (10)

My Favourite Things

Sweets and biscuits are my fave,
Eating, walking through a cave,
At a friend's feeling fine,
Her mum drinking a glass of wine.

Girls Aloud are best by far,
I listen to them in the car,
Into town with all my friends,
They're fun but drive me round the bend.

Buying things fun, fun, fun,
Shops are shutting, time to run,
Lots of clothes for me to wear,
One top came with a cuddly bear.

Playing with friends, eating buns,
Sleepovers when the day is done,
But chill out time is the best,
Time to finally get some rest.

Back home feeling tired,
Hope that chicken hasn't expired,
Messing with channels on TV,
Getting to sleep quite happily.

Livvy Chester (11)

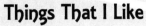

Things That I Like

I like Ferrari cars
And chocolate bars,
And Walkers crisps
And PG Tips.
I like the colour blue
And my designer K Swiss shoes.
I like watching Phinias and Ferb,
It's superb.
I like my song lyrics,
They're terrific.
I like to play games
That keep me entertained.
I like to keep healthy,
Oh Lord, let me be wealthy!
I support Manchester United,
I like to keep my hopes up and I'm always excited.
On a stage I would love to sing,
On my small finger is a diamond ring.
I like to race and run, run, run,
My handy motto is fun, fun, fun!

Ali Lone (12)

My Favourite Things Poem

Tae kwon do
Gives me a smile,
It's much better than
Running a mile.

Watching TV,
Playing video games,
Reading a book,
Are some of my favourite things.

I can't wait
To get home and play,
So I can do my favourite things
Every day.

Going outside
And playing baseball,
Also basketball,
Although I'm not tall.

Playing with friends,
Inside and out,
Not seeing them long enough
Will make me pout.

I have many hobbies,
Like Warhammer 40K,
It's very fun to play,
Even on a Saturday.

This favourite things poem
Has finally ended.
At first I thought I couldn't think of anything,
But then I decided to mend it.

Gil Torten (10)

The Seasons

In spring blossom falls on my head,
Quiet at night when I go to bed.
Pink and white all over the trees,
What a wonderful sight for you to see.

In spring, blossom could decorate cakes,
It wants me to add some chocolate flakes.
New animals begin to be born,
Smells like fresh sweetcorn.

In summer the sun smiles at me,
In a garden of flowers, what a great place to be!
Ice cream melting drip by drip,
Some is melting on my lips.

In autumn the wind blows fast,
Leaves dancing their way to the grass.
Fallen leaves of yellow, orange and brown,
The wind whispers a secret so loud.

In winter ice cracks underneath me,
Ice skating on the lake, a nice place to be.
Playing in the snow, it's nearly Christmas time,
Presents I've been thinking about in my mind.

Liam Joyce (8)

I Love . . .

I love the thought of bluebirds singing in the tall oak trees,
I love the thought of smiling faces on land and over seas.
I love the thought of great ambitions being successful and achieved,
And I love the thought that I'm on Earth and the amazing friends
and family I receive.

I love the feel of a winter's night when I'm snuggled by a
beaming fire
I love the feel of ocean waves and singing as I desire,
I love the feel of chocolate ice cream melting in my throat
And I love the feel of joyful cheers at Christmas, where my
thoughts just seem to float.

I love the taste of cooked meals with a room full of loving family,
I love the taste of chewy sweets because they make me feel
wild, they make me feel free.
I love the taste of chicken soup when I am ill and need
comforting most,
And I love the taste of my favourite foods when we cheer and
make a toast.

I love the smell of fresh bread as I walk through a baker's door,
I love the smell of spring flowers growing all over the garden floor,
I love the smell of hot chocolate whilst watching a film on a
starry night
And I love the smell of Sunday roast when my face lights up
with delight.

I love the sound of crashing waves on a wonderful
midsummer night,
I love the sound of famous music through my left ear and my right,
I love the sound of a sizzling barbecue when the sun shines throughout
And I love the sound of laughter louder than a shout!

I love the sight of exotic lands on a holiday of a dream,
I love the sight of friendly faces when I am down and we
become a team.
I love the sight of butterflies fluttering as happy as can be,
And I love the sight of other people enjoying these sights with me.

I love being in a world of my own when I'm on the beach,
Sun in my face, sand through my toes and wind in my hair.
I love being different, my smile, my hair, my eyes, my style,

My thoughts and my loves, because being different is special
and you shouldn't have to care!

I love the thought of blue birds singing in the tall oak trees,
I love the thought of smiling faces on land and over seas,
I love the thought of great ambitions being successful and achieved,
And I love the thought that I'm on Earth and the amazing friends
and family I receive.

Cherise Harris (13)

My Favourite Things

Laptops, clothes, shoes and more,
Animals that roar until they're sore,
Friends that fight make me mad,
And then I get very sad.
Parties and holidays with my friends and family
Are the best gifts anyone could give me.
Money, money, money, I love money,
But before you know it, it's all gone!

Rhiannon Rose (12)

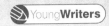

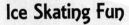

Ice Skating Fun

I grip to the side,
Careful I might slide,
While my knife-like blades
Slice through the icy lake.
A cold shiver creeps up my back,
Like a horrible spider, all hairy and black.
I begin to slip and slide,
But then I twirl and glide.
I really wish I was a figure skater,
But I know that will come much, much later.
Even though it's just a dream,
I love ice skating - it's so supreme!

Rainbow Sweet (10)

My Favourite Things

I do like eating,
But I'm very slow.
Fish is my favourite
And it helps my brain grow and grow.

My bike makes me feel peaceful,
But not on the road.
Clothes are comfortable,
But overall family and friends are loveable.

Swimming is fun and I like
To cut through the waves, like a knife does to butter.
Dancing is also great because it makes me feel free,
Until I fall over and bash my knee.

I love to go on holiday,
Especially to Spain,
But once when I went,
It rained and rained.

Georgina Cartlich (9)

Gymnastics

Up in the morning - I'm ready to go,
To swing on the bar, to and fro.
Will I fall? I never know!

Up on the beam, keeping my balance,
Then onto the floor, showing my talents.
Flipping myself over the vault,
Then landing with a present and a halt!

Achieving things no one can do,
Trying my best so no one will boo.
Competition time has come,
I'm looking my best and having fun.
Gold medal - *yes, I've won!*

Now it's finished, I'm going to rest,
Knowing that I have done my best!

Courtney Sweet (12)

My Favourite Thing

Music's my life, music's my game,
In every lyric, in every name.

See it, hear it, touch it or smell it,
Sing it, love it, feel it and spell it.

I love to sing, it's in my blood,
Listen to my iPod around the neighbourhood.

Dancing is fun, I love that too,
Along to the beat, one-two, one-two.

Music is cool, it's one of the best,
I play the piano, there's simply no test.

Music's my life, music's my game,
In every lyric, in every name.

Paige McDermott (12)

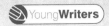

I Like To . . .

I like to act and sing and dance,
Whenever I have the slightest chance.
I like to jog and run and swim,
Every week I'm at the gym.

I like to lie out in the sun,
Once the summer has begun.
I like to lay with my pet bunny,
Sometimes I even feed him honey.

I like to read lots of books,
Sometimes I get funny looks.
I like to paint and colour and draw,
After that I have to do more.

Hannah Fretton (14)

Dogs Are My Favourite Things

Dogs really are my favourite type of pet,
All have noses which really are quite wet.

Their breed is not that important to me,
As long as I can sit them on my knee.

I have a puppy, his name is called Twix.
He's a retriever and red setter mix.

When I am bigger in so many ways,
I'll work at the kennel, caring for strays.

I like to teach Twix a trick or two,
The reward is a bone he can chew.

There is quite a lot for a dog I'll do,
Other than cleaning up fresh piles of poo!

Lydia Hill (10)

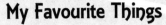

My Favourite Things

Playing Nintendo and watching the telly,
While eating jam doughnuts (they go straight to my belly!)
Bobbing my head to a tune when I sing,
These are a few of my favourite things.

Going on holiday and smiling in the sun,
Messing with my dad and also my mum!
Playing with shells which the sea brings,
These are a few of my favourite things.

Colouring pictures with all my pens,
Having lots of fun with all of my friends!
Making collages with glue, card and string,
These are a few of my favourite things.

When my dog bites, and the cut stings,
I'll be feeling sad,
I simply remember all these lovely things
And then I don't feel so bad!

Marisol Smith (9)

My Favourite Things

I like reading
That is full of meaning
It is great fun
When you read eating a bun
Reading gives us knowledge
Both in and out of college
Reading is extremely good
For the entire brotherhood.

Dulashna Ferdinando (9)

Favourite Things I Do

Arty and crafty stuff I do,
By using coloured paper and glue.
Sketching and shading I do a lot,
By using designs and dots.

Netball and football I like to play,
But hope the weather's not too grey.
Other sports I too do like,
As well as riding my bike.

Gadgets and computer games I like a lot,
MP3 and more I have got,
But cannot forget the weather outside,
Something not similar to the inside.

Writing poems and reading books,
Books which not always can be recognised
                        from the cover's look.
Writing stories, another thing,
Mostly about Queens or even Kings.

Going to school, the best,
Learning, enjoying and having a jest,
Learning something new every day,
As we listen and say.

Helping Mum and Dad,
As I always have,
Cooking or tidying up or more,
With fun and glory.

Smital Dhake (11)

Favourite Things

Water to swim in,
Flumes to ride in,
Boards to dive from,
Oh how good it is for splashing,
That's why swimming is a favourite thing.

Up and down,
Round and round,
You can do tricks too.
Oh how good it is for bouncing,
That's why trampoline is a favourite thing.

Bouncing on the floor,
It goes swish in the hoop,
You jump to dunk
And you jump to score,
That's why basketball is a favourite thing.

At my skate park,
A tail will whip,
With a backflip within it,
That's why BMXing is a favourite thing.

So these are a few of my favourite things.

Sam Selvage (13)

113

My Favourite Things

Teddy bears, teddy bears,
Scruffy or neat,
You all have to share
Under the sheet.

Teddy bears, teddy bears,
Big or small,
They all have paws
To throw a ball.

Teddy bears, teddy bears,
White or brown,
They all deeply care
But do not make a sound.

Teddy bears, teddy bears,
I love them all!

Maisie Fitzgerald (9)

My Favourite Things

Fishing, football and making cakes,
Eating chocolate ice cream, holding my snake.
Going to the zoo, watching the monkeys swing,
These are a few of my favourite things.

Cai Bentley (9)
Darlinghurst Primary & Nursery School, Leigh on Sea

My Favourite Things

Playing with my paintball gun,
Getting new toys is very fun.
Buying a watch and bling,
These are a few of my favourite things.

Playing football, scoring goals,
Eating sweets in a bowl,
Adding sums, my bird that sings,
These are a few of my favourite things.

Ollie Halpin
Darlinghurst Primary & Nursery School, Leigh on Sea

My Favourite Things

Playing with Lego, having fun,
Scoring a try in rugby, we won,
Watching the air show, bright red wings,
These are a few of my favourite things.

Brendon Taylor (9)
Darlinghurst Primary & Nursery School, Leigh on Sea

My Favourite Things

Swimming with my friends,
Reading never ends,
Going to the woods, hearing birds sing,
These are a few of my favourite things.

Doing my spy group
And playing with hula hoops,
Making jewellery out of beads and strings,
These are a few of my favourite things.

Lauren Tobin (9)
Darlinghurst Primary & Nursery School, Leigh on Sea

My Favourite Things

Running and skipping are nice to do,
Going to the cinema, oh what a queue!
Having fresh air and hearing the birds sing,
These are a few of my favourite things.

Jamieleigh Manging (9)
Darlinghurst Primary & Nursery School, Leigh on Sea

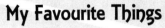

My Favourite Things

Jelly on my plate,
Oh yummy in my tummy,
Scrummy, scrummy, scrummy!
Castles, knights and kings,
These are a few of my favourite things.

Gadgets, gizmos and magic,
Doctor Who,
Stuff that pings,
These are a few of my favourite things.

Sam Collins (8)
Darlinghurst Primary & Nursery School, Leigh on Sea

Holiday

Holiday!
Sunny skies,
Sea and sand,
Water park, adventure day,
Running, sliding, splashing, laughing, fun,
Hot crepes with sauce,
Joking, journey home,
Stunning sunset,
Happiness.

Jack Whitaker (11)
Gayhurst School, Gerrards Cross

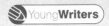

My Favourite Thing

My favourite thing is a terrible thing,
It snorts and growls
Like a hungry bear.
It shouts and cries
Like a boy in pain,
It shoves and kicks
Like a kangaroo.
It moans and groans
Like an ugly ogre.
My mum told me to kiss her,
And my favourite thing is . . . *my sister!*

Omar Hatteea (10)
Gayhurst School, Gerrards Cross

My Favourite Things

I like to sit down and build Lego,
I like to play with it too.
I like to relax with a good book,
I hope these things interest you.

I enjoy the sweet taste of chocolate,
The way that it melts on your tongue.
I enjoy a fun singing session,
And I like a good song to be sung.

I like to play games on my DS,
I like to play Nintendo Wii,
But of all of these, the one I choose
Has got to be family!

Matthew Maynard (11)
Gayhurst School, Gerrards Cross

Trees

Oak and elm,
Pine and fur,
All incredible,
All amazing.
Spiky leaves,
Needles, lopped,
Round and prickly,
Without them,
Without paper,
Without them,
Without us.

Jamie Hinch (11)
Gayhurst School, Gerrards Cross

My Favourite Thing

My favourite game
Is my Wii,
Because it's exercise
You see.

Myself and Ben,
We play together,
So we don't care
If it's bad weather.

We're nice and warm
And having a laugh,
Until Mum shouts,
'It's time for a bath.'

Once we start,
We cannot stop.
I hope this poem
Wins me a laptop!

Chloe Jessop (10)
Limpsfield Junior School, Sheffield

My Favourite Things

A warm mug of cocoa on an icy winter's day,
A cold ice cube shivering down my bony back,
These are a few of my favourite things.

Puff pastry rising higher and higher,
The fresh scent of flowers filling the air,
These are a few of my favourite things.

The soft wind whistling in the calm air,
Clean bed quilts layered on top of me,
These are a few of my favourite things.

Sweet-smelling perfume surrounding the room,
The spectacular sight of a beautiful, multicoloured rainbow,
These are *all* of my favourite things!

Chloe Coombs (9)
Limpsfield Junior School, Sheffield

My Favourite Thing!

H ysterical blazing beach
O ceans waving as I surf
L emonade trickling down my throat
I ce cream melting in the sultry sun
D elicious treats vanishing by the second
A fter night, we are out!
Y elling and screaming in the arcades
S undown has come, time to leave!

Kimberly Hewitt Hind (9)
Limpsfield Junior School, Sheffield

My Favourite Things

A lligators anxiously awaiting their prey
N ightingales nicely humming away
I guanas in the desert's ray
M onkeys messing all of the day
A nts around the picnic buffet
L eopards leaping - it's time to play
S uch sweet things we see today!

Marvin Morton (10)
Limpsfield Junior School, Sheffield

I Like To . . .

I like to run a mile or two,
I once ran up to Chester Zoo!

I like to skip up and down,
Jumping over 'lost and found'!

I like to cycle round and round,
I'd even ride right into town!

I like to walk along the shore,
How can this ever be a bore?

I like to move it!

Zoe Mullen (10)
Limpsfield Junior School, Sheffield

My Favourite Things

My favourite things are
Jumping up and down,
Or going shopping in town.

My favourite things are
To play with my brother,
Or do some learning with my mother.

My favourite things are
Going to school
Or going out and staying cool.

My favourite things are
To play on my Nintendo,
Or cut shapes out of cookie dough.

Finally, my favourite things are
To get ready for bed
And curl up with my favourite ted.

Khateejah Bibi (10)
Limpsfield Junior School, Sheffield

My Favourite Thing!

S unbathing, while the sun beats down on my back
U mbrellas shading me as I relax
M elting ice cream melting in my mouth
M unching on delicious rock
E xciting weather every day
R aining is not going to happen today.

Chloe Birch (10)
Limpsfield Junior School, Sheffield

My Favourite Things

M anuella and Chloe are my hysterical friends
Y oyo revolving at River Thames

F loating through my ballet dance
A nts nibbling through my pants
V anilla may be unusual, but I'm flexible
O ther things I love, like my dad's floppy belly is shakeable
U nited Kingdom is magnificent because it's where I live
R ain, wind and snow, in all I play
I n bed is where I lay
T eachers nagging in my face
E ars help me listen when I tie my lace

T owels help me get dry
H owever I like delicious meat and potato pie
I ce is cool, I could freeze up in an ice cube
N othing can stop me singing
G ymnastics is my thing
S oon as I play table tennis I have to say pong ping!

Connie Horne (10)
Limpsfield Junior School, Sheffield

My Favourite Things

My favourite things are
Taking my dog out for a walk to the pier,
He takes a run and jumps,
Then he goes for a swim.

I also like going on rides on my bike,
With my dad and Craig,
Although I am faster than them,
It is still good fun.

I like to help my mum to cook the dinner,
My favourite thing is
Cutting the carrots,
But they are disgusting!

I like swimming in the deep end
And splashing my dad,
He splashes me back
And so it goes on.

These are all my favourite things
But also doing the gardening,
Pulling the weeds and plant flowers,
They are all my favourite things.

Molly Erskine (8)
Paible School, North Uist

133

My Favourite Things

My favourite things are
Playing with my pet,
Playing with my Nintendo DS,
Going to the beach, in the sea,
Cycling on my bike,
Doing tricks on my brother.

Watching SpongeBob SquarePants,
Going to my cousin's house,
Going to the shop for sweets,
Playing on my brother's PSP,
Going shopping with my mum.
These are all my favourite things!

Joanna MacBain (10)
Paible School, North Uist

Can't You Tell My Favourite Things?

My name is Esme and I like a nice movie,
High School Musical and others make me groovy.
I like my family and friends too,
But I go to the farm and the cows go moo.
These are my favourite things.

I like elephants, they are so big,
But I also love a big fat pig.
I like to play on the Nintendo Wii,
And run away from a buzzing bee.
These are my favourite things.

Tasty ice cream is the best,
I think it is better than all the rest.
Singing to music and having fun
Is better than eating a hot cross bun.
These are my favourite things, especially in the sun.

Chocolate cake I like the most,
And walking along the beautiful coast.
I like biscuits, they are so yummy,
But I love how they fill your tummy.
Are these your favourite things?

Esme Howarth (11)
St Mary Magdalen's CE Primary School, Accrington

My Favourite Things

I like jumping on a trampoline,
One day I wish I could meet the Queen,
My favourite subject has to be Art and DT,
And I like swimming in the sea.

My favourite sweet is a dib-dab,
I like spending time with my dad,
And taking the dogs for a walk in the park,
I don't even get annoyed when they bark!

I also like surfing the Net
And sometimes going on Marapets,
In football I'm always in the goal,
And I save all those footballs.

I have two mates, they are the best,
They help me through all my tests.
Me and Hannah we practically live together,
And Emily's nice, whatever the whether.

I like going in town with my friends,
My favourite car is a Mercedes Benz,
I have five people in my family,
My mum, my dad, my two sisters and me!

Jessica Williams (11)
St Mary Magdalen's CE Primary School, Accrington

My Favourite Things!

A gift of love,
It's right above.
A ball of fun,
The sun,
The sun!

It's on the sea,
Not like me.
It's just the thought,
A boat,
A boat!

Like a game of life,
I want a wife.
To include them all,
Football,
Football!

Thomas Bartley (11)
St Mary Magdalen's CE Primary School, Accrington

My Favourite Foods!

I like to eat
A lot of sweets,
Beans on toast
I like the most!

Pizza and chips,
Oranges with pips,
All sorts of foods
In all different moods!

An explosion of flavours,
My favourite crisps are Quavers,
All these foods are the best,
So much better than the rest!

Cory Foster (11)
St Mary Magdalen's CE Primary School, Accrington

Hamsters And Pets

H amsters are the best!
A nimals are so cute
M ost pets are the best
S mall, but cute
T oys for pets make them happy
E ver and ever they will make you happy
R abbits and hamsters are cute
S mall, but fast!

Jordan Gamble (10)
St Mary Magdalen's CE Primary School, Accrington

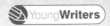

My Favourite Things!

Running alone, wind in my hair,
Running in winter, I can bear.
Swimming in galas as fast as I can,
Going on holiday, coming back with a tan,
Hitting a shuttlecock just with a swing,
Seeing a bird's beautiful wing.

So listen up, this is my future,
When I grow up I want to be a lawyer.
After university, after college,
I want to get a degree,
This is as simple as ABC.

I like to watch Disney, volume high,
But I dislike having to say goodbye.
I go to mosque as well as school,
All my family are totally cool.

This is my family, Mum, Dad and sis,
Embarrassingly they always give me a kiss,
Especially my parents.

My favourite fruit is a peach,
My favourite place is the beach.

Whatever the weather, this is me.

Amina Mulla (11)
St Mary Magdalen's CE Primary School, Accrington

My Favourite Things

Me, my friends, my family too,
Have lots of things that we can do.
Most of these things make me happy,
Even though I have to change my brother's nappy.

Every day I'm always at school,
But sometimes we go to the swimming pool.
I go down town with my mates,
I open the gate, it is so great.

These are my favourite subjects at school,
Art, DT, they are so cool.
Football, netball, they are fun,
For my dinner I had an iced bun.

Hannah Durkin (11)
St Mary Magdalen's CE Primary School, Accrington

YoungWriters

what are your
favourite
things?

Write about your favourite things for our new poetry competition. Send us your poem for the chance to be published and even win your very own laptop!

PlayStation games and **playing in the sun**
Visiting friends, **parties**, **holidays** and **fun**
Camping in the garden, **catching things with wings**
Are these a few of your favourite things?

Halloween and **Christmas** – **presents** and **treats**
Watching TV, **eating ice cream** and **sweets**
Going to school, learning about **queens** and **kings**
Are these a few of your favourite things?

A **hug from your mum**, a **kiss from your dad too**
Making stuff out of **coloured paper** and **glue**
Dressing up as a pirate or a **princess with rings**
Are these a few of your favourite things?

Laptops and **gadgets** and **playing with your pet**
Scoring a goal in the back of the net
Babies and **robots** and **puppets with strings**
Are these a few of your favourite things?

X Factor and **reading a good book**
Doing something cheeky then let off the hook
Smiling when **Girls Aloud** or **McFly** sings
Are these a few of your favourite things?

Write your poem, then fill in your name, address and age underneath your poem, place in an envelope and send to us at: My Favourite Things, Young Writers, Remus House, Coltsfoot Drive, Woodston, Peterborough, PE2 9JX. You can email your poem instead to youngwriters@forwardpress.co.uk - don't forget to include your name, age and postal address with My Favourite Things in the subject line.